Training Army Al

By Sheila Sweeny Higginson

Based on an episode by Chris Nee

Based on the series created by Chris Nee

Illustrated by Character Building Studio and the Disney Storybook Artists

SUSTAINABLE FORESTRY INITIATIVE

Certified Chain of Custody
Promoting Sustainable Forestry

www.sfiprogram.org
SFI-01415
The SFI label applies to the text stock

DISNEY PRESS
New York • Los Angeles

The weekend of the Badger Scout campout has finally arrived. Donny and Dad are busy packing. One brave toy will join Donny. "Whichever toy you bring should have a doctor's note clearing it for the trip," Doc tells her brother.
She offers to check out all the toys.

3

Doc gathers the toys in her bedroom.
"Toys, we've got a situation," she says.

"Oh, no! Not a situation!" Stuffy cries. "Uh, what's a situation?"
"Donny needs one toy to go with him on his Badger Scout camping trip this weekend," Doc explains.

Teddy B remembers his trip with Donny last year.
"I got dropped in a puddle and dragged through leaves, and I had to sleep stuffed in the bottom of a sleeping bag," he says, shuddering.

Lambie, Hallie, and Stuffy don't want to go to the campout, either.
Neither does Sir Kirby, Bronty, Squeakers, or Chilly.

Then Doc sees one brave toy's hand raised in the air.
"Army Al, reporting for duty," Donny's toy soldier says.

"I don't want my best friend to go!" Bronty cries.
"Sorry, buddy," Army Al replies. "I'm a soldier. I was made to serve. I'm the right toy for this mission."

Doc gives Army Al his pre-trip checkup.
The toy soldier's heartbeat is marching right along.
His eyes and ears are working perfectly.
Army Al is in great shape.

Doc is ready to present her diagnosis.
"You have a case of the Ready-to-Serves," she says. "As soon as you're done with basic training, you'll be ready for active duty."

It's basic training time! Doc and the toys prepare Army Al for anything the scouts might throw at him.
Teddy B gives Al the stinky-shoe test.
Al gets a little teary, but he passes with flying colors.

Sir Kirby and Stuffy pull Army Al in all directions.

Hallie covers him with sticky marshmallow goo.

But Al aces every challenge. He will do anything to protect and serve his fellow toys.

Army Al has completed toy boot camp.
"Soldier, I'm really impressed with the kind of toy you are on the inside,"
Doc says. "You're all heart and willing to sacrifice to make life better for
all of us. And that's the best kind of toy to be."

Army Al is ready to serve at Donny's campout! Lambie gives him three cuddles to hold on to in case of a cuddle emergency.

Doc carries Al outside and helps him into Donny's backpack.
Then she waves good-bye to Dad, Donny, and Army Al.

Army Al's toughness is put to the test all weekend.

Donny and Luca play catch with him.
The Badger Scouts hang him upside down.

They twist his arms and legs until he looks like a pretzel.

But it isn't all hard work.
At night, Army Al gets to snuggle next to Donny in his sleeping bag.

At the end of the weekend, Dad and Donny return home.
Army Al is grimy, but it looks like he's still in one piece.
"I'd better take him for a checkup," Doc tells Donny.

Inside the clinic, the toys can't wait to hear about the campout. "It was tough, but fun!" Army Al reports. "And most of all, I was ready for it, thanks to all your training!"

Hallie steps forward with a homemade medal. "In honor of all you do for us, and the fact that you're braver than a bunny in a basket of bobcats, we award you the Medal of Toy Bravery," she says.

Doc pins the medal on Army Al.
Then Doc and all the toys salute the incredibly brave toy soldier.

"At ease, soldier," Doc says with a smile. "And welcome home!"